RUTH-EMMA
HERSELF

Karin Stjernholm Ræder

RUTH-EMMA HERSELF

translated by Patricia Crampton

KESTREL BOOKS

KESTREL BOOKS
Published by Penguin Books Ltd
Harmondsworth, Middlesex, England

Copyright © 1977 by Karin Stjernholm Ræder
Translation Copyright © 1981 by Patricia Crampton

First published in Great Britain by Kestrel Books 1981
Originally published in Sweden as *Rut-Emma Själv* by
Carlsen 1977

ISBN 0 7226 5727 7

Printed in Great Britain by Richard Clay
(The Chaucer Press) Ltd, Bungay, Suffolk

*To those who played in the
same backyard as I did.
(And to those who played in other
backyards, too. After all, one
backyard is as good as another.)*

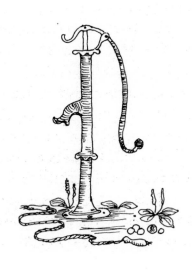

This is where we live. We have a water-pump,
but it's rusty and doesn't work any more.

7

Old Mr Nilsson has his workshop in the yard.
He makes clogs.

8

Mr Nilsson is probably the only person who knows that I'm not as stupid as I look. We talk about all kinds of things. His mouth is full of little tacks, but he can still talk. Every so often he takes some tacks out and hammers a bit of leather on to a wooden sole. He paints the leather black and it smells nice. Sometimes he paints on a green border as well.

One day he gave me a little of the green paint in a tin, and a beautiful, clean paintbrush. When I went up to our kitchen I saw a cake with white

icing on the table. It looked freshly baked. Someone had put water on the stove for coffee, but no one was there.

I desperately wanted to paint something with my green paint and the clean little paintbrush. That white icing would look absolutely wonderful with something painted on it. So I painted a big green sun on the cake, and then a green flower in the middle of the sun. It really did look rather nice, but I got my nails all green because the paint was so runny.

Then Mum and Aunt Emma and Grandma came in. They were very cross and said the paint was poisonous.

'Let's see if we can get the icing off,' they said. 'Perhaps the rest will be all right.'

But the paint had gone right down into the cake.

'We'll have to throw the whole cake away,' they said. 'We might be poisoned. It could be very dangerous.'

They told me to take the cake down to the yard and throw it in the dustbin. It seemed such a shame. I'm usually told that you shouldn't throw food away when so many people go to bed hungry. I hoped Mr Nilsson wouldn't see me.

Uncle Oscar's dog, whose name is Bob, was sitting by the dustbin, watching me. Bob is about the only person who likes me. He's rather fat and very comfortable to sit beside.

I thought there might be a bit of cake which wasn't green, so I broke it up and had a look. There were several pieces which had no paint on them at all and Bob and I shared them. We sat down to eat by the dustbin. The cake tasted lovely and Bob licked his nose and looked at me with his kind, damp eyes.

It was my turn to do the washing-up that day. Nobody helped me to dry.

You can see down into the yard from the kitchen window. I suddenly thought that perhaps Bob and I might have swallowed some of that poisonous paint after all, although I'd looked at every bit we ate. My tummy began to feel rather funny. I thought about Bob, who's always so

kind, and I felt my chin shrinking and my nose
tingling and the tears began to well up into my
eyes and drip down into the sink.

But afterwards, when I'd finished the
washing-up, I forgot to wonder how my tummy
was feeling.

'Blow your nose,' they said. 'Tie up your shoe
laces,' they said, as they always do. And I did.
And after that everything was the same as usual.

13

My big sister's name is Ingeborg. She has dark corkscrew curls and blue eyes. She's awfully pretty, everyone says so. Ingeborg goes to junior school. One day she came home with a star made of gold paper, because she could write such beautiful letters.

I'd really love to have a gold star like that!

She has a hymn book with a lovely bookmark of an angel.

My little sister has curls too, but they're fair.

Her name is Madeleine. I always have Ingeborg's clothes passed down to me, but after I've had them they're worn out, Mum says, so Madeleine gets new ones. That's why she's always so pretty and looks like a doll.

My name is Ruth, after Grandma. My second name is Emma, after Aunt Emma. When someone I don't know asks what my name is I sometimes say, 'Ruth-Emma.' At least it sounds a little better than just Ruth. My hair is absolutely straight.

One day Mum twisted all my hair up in curl papers. Then I had curly hair which bounced when I walked. But next day it was straight again. Well, at least I can remember how it felt.

Sometimes Mum asks, 'Can't you put your slide in properly? Try and sew your button on

yourself. Do up your shoe laces!' she says. But if
you're always doing that kind of thing you never
have any time left to sit and think.

I like to sit and think with Bob. You can sit
and think and remember about things which
happened a long time ago. The very first thing I
remember is when Dad ran away with the circus.
Mum was as mad as a bee. She took down all the
photographs we had with Dad in them, but when
she took down the big photograph which hung
over the chest of drawers, the wallpaper
underneath was torn, so she put it back again. It
was a good thing she did, because otherwise I
don't think I would have remembered what Dad
looked like at all.

I don't know exactly what Dad does in the
circus. We're never allowed to talk about him,
because Mum gets as mad as a bee again.
Sometimes I think he does tricks on a trapeze. I
think I'll do tricks on a trapeze when I'm grown

17

up. I'm going to run away and join the circus too, and Dad and I can do tricks together. We can turn somersaults and jump about high up in the air, and then everyone will think we're awfully clever.

That's the sort of thing I sit and think about with Bob. I miss Dad sometimes. If he were here perhaps I'd like him as much as I like Bob. And Bob is my favourite person in the whole world.

Inside the yard gates there's a doorway leading to Uncle Oscar's shop. Most of the things Uncle Oscar sells are boring, but sometimes, when he decides it looks like spring, he puts some skipping-ropes and a bowl of marbles on the counter.

And at Christmas time he fetches a pile of cardboard boxes with dolls inside from the cellar. We found the dolls one day when it was raining and we weren't allowed to stay indoors and play and it was boring just standing by the yard gates.

Neither Ingeborg nor I play with dolls any more, but there is a special thrill about playing with a brand-new doll, fixed in a box. We opened box after box. Some of the dolls had golden-yellow hair and some shiny black and when you stood them upright they opened their eyes with a little click. Two of them were wearing baby clothes and had a gap between their lips, so we went up to the kitchen for some rice to poke in the hole.

We could have gone on playing with them for ages, if Uncle Oscar hadn't come in and found us.

He said we'd ruined his dolls and that they weren't brand-new any more.

'Who wants to buy dolls stuffed with rice, I ask you?' he cried, looking very cross and he locked the cellar door.

'Please keep an eye on your children,' he said to Mum when we went upstairs.

Mum was hard at work painting angels, as usual. The ones she thought specially good she put to dry on the stairs where everyone could see them. Uncle Oscar says that Mum thinks she's going to be world-famous one day for her beautiful angels.

Of course Mum was also angry with us because we'd played with Uncle Oscar's dolls.

'Can't you ever be trusted?' she said. 'This is dreadful. What am I to do?'

Then she put all the angels in a basket and told us to take them to a shop near by.

'Take Madeleine with you so that she doesn't get up to any mischief,' said Mum. 'And don't clump down the stairs like that!' she called after us, although we were jumping beautifully, on the very tips of our toes.

At the shop they make the angels into candlesticks and send back new, unpainted ones.

It was still raining. Ingeborg put out the palm of her hand to feel the rain and said, 'It doesn't matter. It'll soon stop.'

Madeleine, who is always copying, put out her dirty little hand too. A lady who was passing, stopped and said, 'Are you selling those beautiful angels? Poor little girl, are you cold?' she asked, looking at Madeleine who was standing there with her dirty, outstretched hand and her red and running nose.

'Here you are,' said the nice lady, and put a whole 10p piece in Madeleine's hand, which she was holding so neatly cupped that the coin fitted perfectly inside it.

We were really surprised when we realized that the lady thought Madeleine was a beggar.

But if you looked carefully, perhaps Madeleine did look rather poor.

'Shall we go shares?' asked Ingeborg, and Madeleine, who was always pleased when she was allowed to be with us, said, 'Yes, of course,' straight away.

All the way home we stopped and looked in shop windows, trying to decide what to buy. Finally we reached Uncle Oscar's boring windows. There was nothing we wanted there, because he hadn't put out the marbles yet. He still didn't think it looked like spring.

Then I had a good idea: we could hide the 10p until Christmas and when Uncle Oscar brought the dolls up from the cellar we could go into his shop and buy a lovely doll in a box.

'We like the ones with rice in,' we'd say. Uncle Oscar *would* be surprised.

Sometimes, when everyone is being stupid and no one in the whole world cares about me, I sit

and think about my Dad. If I hurry up and learn those trapeze artists' tricks I can run away from home and find the circus and go with it.

So I began to practise turning somersaults.

Down in the yard there's an iron railing in front of the windows which is just the right height. It feels dangerous at first, but after a while it's easy.

One day when Ingeborg came home from school I asked her if she'd like to run away with me. I didn't want to be unfriendly and go away on my own. Ingeborg just sniffed. She didn't think Dad was still with the circus at all. But she was awfully good at turning somersaults.

Ingeborg does everything better than I do.

27

In the backyard next to ours lives a boy called Theo. He sometimes comes in and plays with us. I think Theo is the handsomest boy I know. How I'd love to join in and play when he comes! But he only wants to be with Ingeborg.

One day he came and watched while we turned somersaults. I spun round as beautifully as I possibly could, but Theo didn't see me at all. He just said to Ingeborg, 'You look like a real circus princess!'

Theo, I said in my silent inside voice, can't you see that *I'm* the circus princess?

But he couldn't hear my inside voice and began to turn somersaults himself. Then he did a handstand. Theo was fantastic.

'Oh you are clever, Theo,' said Ingeborg, laughing an elegant film-star laugh and tossing her head to make the corkscrew curls bob up and down.

Theo looked awfully pleased and his cheeks turned a little red.

I wanted to please Theo too.

'Theo, you are clever,' I said, just like Ingeborg. 'Perhaps we could perform at the circus and you could come too.'

And then I laughed a film-star laugh as well.

Theo roared with laughter and said, 'You can do a special act, spitting cherry stones out through that gap!'

Well really! Sometimes you can get really furious with Theo, even though he is very handsome!

Then Ingeborg and Theo went over to Theo's yard and skipped with the others who lived there. There is a little door in the wall between the yards and you can watch from there. They're awfully good at skipping. They stand in a line and run forward, skip and shout 'whizz' and skip even faster. It looks difficult. I don't think I shall ever learn to skip – not 'whizz', anyway.

When it's warm Madeleine spends all day in the yard behind a crate, playing schools.

She has a rabbit called Peter and a doll called Tissy. When we ask her what she's doing she says she's busy.

'Shush, don't disturb me,' she says.

Then she starts whispering to Peter and Tissy.

Sometimes there are little dead baby birds lying under the big tree in the yard. If you've got a small cigar box you can bury them in the flowerbed but it's not so much fun when you're on your own.

Ingeborg has swopped her angel bookmark in the hymn book for a cross with forget-me-nots round it. Forget-me-nots are her favourite flowers.

'What's your favourite flower?' she asked me once, but I didn't know.

'What's your next favourite flower?' I asked her.

'Violets,' she said. She always knows the answer, whatever you ask.

The next time she asks me what my favourite flower is, I'm going to say violets. I'm going to ask for a cross with violets round it when I have a hymn book.

Mr Nilsson has his window open. He says spring has arrived.

Uncle Oscar put up two swings in the entrance to the warehouse. One of them was a baby swing for Madeleine. The other one was a real trapeze. It felt wonderful, swinging to and fro with my hair flying. Then I leant right back, but somehow I slipped and fell off. That *was* a hard bump! It hurt so much that I was sure I'd have to cry, but I didn't.

'You haven't got a nose,' said Madeleine, looking sad.

'Has it come off?' For a moment I was afraid it had come off. I got blood on my fingers when I felt for it.

Then Ingeborg and Theo came out and said, 'Get out of the way, we want to have a go!'

And Theo said, 'You look like a clown now, with that red nose. It'll go well with your circus act!'

Oh, Theo can be absolutely unbearable!

One day Theo said he'd seen a poster outside the tobacconist's saying there was a circus in town.

I was really happy.

'Did you hear that?' I said to Ingeborg. 'The circus is here. We must go and see Dad!'

35

But Ingeborg shrugged her shoulders in her snooty way and said, 'You don't really think that Dad will be there, do you, stupid?'

But of course I did.

'You're a silly baby,' she said, 'and you know quite well that Mum won't let us go to the circus.'

Of course I did know that.

'Why don't you think Dad will be there?' I said.

'There are lots of circuses,' Ingeborg scoffed. 'In any case, I think Dad has gone back to sea.'

Ingeborg says Dad was the mate on a ship before he ran away to the circus. Ingeborg pretends she knows everything, just because she's the eldest.

'I'm going anyway,' I said, and I tried to look snooty, too.

Ingeborg and Theo stood up on the trapeze, swinging. It looked clever and dangerous. They weren't listening any more. Madeleine shouted, 'Me and Peter and Tissy think you're the cleverest people in the world!'

If only I had the money to buy a ticket, I could go without asking anyone, I thought. I was sure Dad would be there. Perhaps he was a *lion-tamer* at the circus, I thought. I wondered how to get the money for the ticket.

If you keep on and on thinking, you nearly always get a good idea in the end. Remember that lady who gave Madeleine a whole 10p because she thought Madeleine was a poor little beggar girl? Well, I was just thinking about her.

Madeleine is always a good sport and likes to help. When I asked her, she said yes at once. But how was I to get Madeleine to look pathetic, now it wasn't so cold out any more?

I would have to take off her shoes and socks and put her into something shabby, I thought. I had a cardigan with holes in the elbows. It was rather dirty, too.

We stood on the corner of the square and Madeleine put out her hand and held it like a little bowl in the way she does so well.

Several people were very sorry for Madeleine and put money in her little hand. I took the

money away at once and put it in the marbles'
bag I had brought with me, so that it wouldn't
get lost.

'What are you doing here, children?' said a
lady I recognized. 'Aren't you Esther's little
girls?'

'We're so cold and hungry,' I said.

The lady looked angry and said, 'Stop
pretending!'

She went away, and came back a little later
with Aunt Emma.

'We were only playing,' I said.

But Madeleine started to howl like she sometimes does and the tears squirted out of her eyes and her nose ran and we had to rush home. It was bad luck for Madeleine who likes being nice and helpful.

When no one was looking, I took the money out of the marbles' bag. It wasn't much.

I went out of the yard gate and then I walked all the way down the High Street and Harbour Road, and down by the harbour I saw the circus tent. It was full of people and flags and horses with beautiful blankets and plumes.

Would I have enough money?

I had to queue for a long time before I got to the ticket office. When I reached it I took out all the money which Madeleine had begged and said, 'Is that enough to buy a ticket?'

'Of course. But it will just be a standing place,' said the lady in the ticket office.

'Would you please let me have a standing place?' I said.

'The show starts in half an hour,' said the ticket lady.

I walked round the tent, with my heart thumping very hard. I was looking for my Dad. I hoped I'd recognize him from the photograph. Anyway, he'd be sure to recognize me, I thought.

There was another entrance at the back of the tent, so I went in there to look. You can't wait for half an hour when you're looking for your Dad. But there were some people there. Some with long cloaks on and others in riding breeches.

'What are you doing here? We're not open yet,' they said.

'I'm looking for Dad,' I said.

'Oh yes, all right then,' they said. 'Are you a circus child?' they asked.

'Of course,' I said.

'You could help us out,' they said. 'You're just right for Evelina's costume, and she's got mumps. Ask your Dad. You've only got to hold on to the end of this garland while little Rosa is riding.'

I was so happy I thought I was going to faint. 'All right, I'll ask,' I said.

'Come back quickly,' they said. 'What have you done to your nose?'

'I fell off the trapeze,' I said.

I walked round for a bit, looking for Dad, but I was afraid I wouldn't find those people in the cloaks and riding breeches again, so I went back almost at once and said, 'Here I am. It's all right.'

'Fine,' they said. 'This is little Rosa,' they said, pointing to a tall girl, 'and here's your costume.'

It was a wonderful costume, a sort of ballet dress. Was I supposed to be a fairy? It had a pink skirt and stuck out and the bodice was made of silver stuff.

'We'll have to put a lot of powder on that nose,' they said. 'Do you know Evelina?'

'Not exactly,' I said.

'We'll give her a wig,' they said, and they put a beautiful curly wig with a pink rose in it on my head.

They gave me a mirror to look at myself in.

'Tuck in that vest that's sticking out,' they said. 'You have to stand here and hold the garland like this. That's all you have to do. It's not too difficult, is it?'

'Not a bit,' I said.

'Good,' they said. 'Stay here. We'll tell you when. Keep still, or you'll spoil the costume.'

Heavens, I was a circus princess! If you've never been one you can't know what it feels like.

The music began to play and some big floodlights were turned on. It smelled wonderful. I stood there, feeling all warm inside. Everything was marvellous.

What about Dad? When would he be coming in? I didn't even know what he'd look like. Would he be on horseback? He might be riding a lion! Dad would be the handsomest man of all, I knew that.

I saw one man in a shiny white silk costume and another in a kind of tiger skin. Was that Dad? Wait till he caught sight of me!

'Keep still,' they hissed in my ear.

There was a clown coming on now but I was too excited to laugh.

Then came the trapeze artist. Could he be Dad? He had fair curly hair. Would he jump down from the trapeze shouting, 'Ruth! What are you doing here?'

But it couldn't have been him. Dad didn't look as young as that in the photograph over the chest of drawers.

Then there was a man who did conjuring tricks. And then they said, 'Stand here now. Don't move. Hold the garland just like this. Show us how well you can do it.'

And the music played and little Rosa came in on a beautiful black horse. Oh, she was wonderful! There was a handsome man in the middle of the ring, wearing a top hat and carrying two long whips which he cracked at the horse.

Was *that* Dad? It could be.

'Is it you?' I shouted, but perhaps he couldn't hear. No one answered. The horse galloped round, throwing up dirt and sand over me. I held on to the garland for all I was worth and everyone clapped and shouted 'Bravo! Bravo!' The horse flew past me again and again. Everything was going round in front of my eyes like when you're on a roundabout.

That must be Dad, the one in the middle, the most splendid man in the whole circus. And little Rosa was splendid, too! She was riding out now and everyone was clapping. It sounded like a tremendous thunderstorm.

They took the garland out of my hand and
said it was over.

Then little Rosa, who had dismounted from
her horse, and the splendid gentleman who
must be Dad ran to the middle of the ring.
She curtsied and he bowed, to thank the
people for applauding.

Oh, they were going off!

But the audience went on clapping. The
curtains were drawn back and they came out
again.

I suddenly thought that I ought to be with them, thanking the audience for applauding. After all, I had been performing too. So I ran forward to join Dad. There I stood, in the light of the big lamps, curtsying with the others. And everyone laughed and clapped.

Now I know what it feels like to be a star, and it suits me perfectly.

Are you my Dad? I wanted to ask, but when I saw him close to, I knew at once that he wasn't.

I wanted to stay there, but they each took me by a hand and ran out, so that I was almost hanging between them like a floating streak.

'Who is she?' the people outside were asking each other. 'Didn't you say your dad was a circus artiste?' they asked me.

'But I can't find him,' I said.

Suddenly Uncle Oscar was there.

'Where is my niece?' he said. 'How could you let her perform! I could hardly believe my eyes!'

Then he said to me, 'How did you get here? Does your mother know about this? She's going to be furious, you know. Hurry up now and I'll take you home. What *do* you think you look like!'

I had to take off my grand dress and my wig. It's not all that easy wearing a wig. It had almost fallen off. It was lucky they had stuck hairpins into it.

They told Uncle Oscar not to be cross.

'She was only there because of a misunderstanding,' they said. 'We do hope you'll overlook it,' they said. 'Our girl got mumps. This is very unfortunate.'

'It certainly is unfortunate,' said Uncle Oscar.

'But where's my Dad?' I asked Uncle Oscar as he marched off with me.

'Did you think he was going to be here?' asked Uncle Oscar.

'Yes,' I said.

He didn't say anything after that and we went home in silence.

At home they behaved as if nothing had happened. No one asked where I'd been, but Grandma got out a jar and rubbed ointment on my nose.

One day I met Theo by the gate and he said,
'Hey Ruth, you're not as silly as I thought.'
Well! All the same, I do like Theo. I think.

A new girl had moved into the house where
Theo lived. I saw her when I was standing by
the door in the wall watching the others skipping.
She was up at the window, watching the
skippers, like me.

They skipped double-throughs and backs and
twists and they were all very good at it. Then
they dropped the rope and ran, because they
were supposed to be rehearsing for the last day
of term and they were going to be late.

The ground was covered with little white flowers from the trees and the birds began to sing now that it was quiet and no one was left.

So I went into Theo's yard and looked around. I don't go there often.

I hadn't been standing there long when the new girl came down, just as if we'd arranged to meet.

'Hallo,' she said. 'Can you skip?'

'No,' I said.

'I can't either,' she said.

'I wonder if we'll ever be able to learn,' I said.
'That's just what I was wondering,' she said.
We looked at the rope lying on the ground. I
knew it was Theo's. You could tie one end to the

door handle and then one person could turn and
the other could skip.

'Shall we have a go?' she said.

'Good idea,' I said.

So we had a go and it was quite difficult. But
it wasn't as tremendously difficult as I had
thought it would be.

'I'm going to junior school next term,' she said.

'Me too,' I said.

'We'll probably be in the same class, then,' she said.

'Great,' I said.

We left Theo's yard and went into our yard and sat down with Bob in the middle and talked.

'I went and performed at the circus once,' I said.

'Did you really?' she said. 'You're not joking? How exciting! That was very daring of you.'

We found a dead baby bird, but we hadn't got a cigar box, so we covered it with flowers instead.

'Shall we be best friends?' she said. 'My name's Elspeth, what's yours?'

She was really pretty. She had little light brown freckles on her nose and a fringe and a dimple in both cheeks. She was about the prettiest girl I'd ever seen.

'My name's Ruth-Emma,' I said.

'Ruth-Emma,' she said, 'what a nice name. I don't know anyone else called that.'

When she had to go I said, 'I'll come with you.'

We skipped all the way back to Theo's yard, the way you do when you feel happy and you've got somebody to skip with. Then we skipped all the way back to my yard again.

'See you tomorrow,' she said.

'See you tomorrow,' I said.

'There's a new girl living in Theo's house,' I told the others, when we were having supper.

'I happen to know that,' said Ingeborg, in that snooty way she has. She always knows everything before anyone else.

'I happen to know that,' said Madeleine, who is always copying.

'I happen to be her best friend,' I said.
That really did surprise them!

Bye, bye.